Magic Magic

STOP CHILDREN

Written by
Delia Huddy

Illustrated by
Sue Heap

WALKER BOOKS
AND SUBSIDIARIES
LONDON · BOSTON · SYDNEY · AUCKLAND

Chapter One

Maggie Magic had been the lollipop lady outside Greengage School for as long as anyone could remember. For years and years and years.

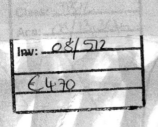

Tina Tipper's grandma had a photo of Tina Tipper's mum when she was a little girl at Greengage School. Maggie looked just the same in that photo: no older, no younger.

"Maggie has magic in her pockets,"
Tina's mum said to Tina. "That's why
she never grows old."

"Of course Maggie's magic," said Tina. "Everybody knows that. Ahmed saw her flying over the supermarket on her lollipop the other evening."

Sometimes Maggie would do a small head-over-heels or stand on her hands.

And she never forgot a birthday – there was always a lollipop in her back pocket.

The children knew the lollipops were magic, because:

(a) they were deliciously fizzy, and

(b) on the day Maggie gave you a lollipop you got all your maths right.

100 × 2 =

5 + 5 = 10

Very good ☆

Chapter Two

One day when
Mr Watkins was crossing
with his son, Sam,
Maggie did a cartwheel.
She caught her foot in
Mr Watkins' pocket and
tore his coat.

Mr Watkins was already in a bad temper because he'd burnt the toast at breakfast time. "Greengage School needs a proper traffic controller," he said. "I shall speak to the headteacher."

The next day, Maggie got a letter.

Greengage
SCHOOL

Dear Maggie,

I have had a serious complaint about your behaviour on crossing patrol.
I am sorry to have to tell you that your services as lollipop lady are no longer wanted.

Yours sincerely,

Mary Biggs

M. Biggs
Headteacher

Mr Grudge was given Maggie's job. He didn't like the children and the children didn't like him.

Everyone at Greengage School was heartbroken. Nobody would speak to Sam Watkins. Not Tina Tipper, Ahmed, Mary P. or Fish Fowler.

Sam was the most heartbroken of all.
He sat down in the playground and cried.
Tina Tipper said, "No good crying over
lost magic. We must do something about
it. I shall call a meeting."

Chapter Three

At playtime they met in the corner of
the playground. All the children came.
"I want ideas!" shouted Tina Tipper.
(She had to shout so that people
at the back could
hear.)

"Down with Mr Watkins!"
screamed Mary P.
"Down with Mr Grudge!"
yelled Fish Fowler.
"I know," said Nisha. "Why don't we sit
on the crossing and refuse to move?"

Tina Tipper looked at Nisha.

"That's a great idea!" she said.

"A sit-down strike! COOL!"

Chapter Four

So that's what happened.
On the day of the strike,
every single pupil joined in
– and many of the parents
came as well. The crowd
stretched right across the
road and all the way to
the shops.

Tina Tipper's mum brought a large
umbrella to keep off the sun, and
a bag filled with chocolate biscuits
for playtime, cheese rolls and pizza
for lunch, and iced buns for tea.

Ahmed's family, who had a shop by the school, gave everyone cups of tea and cold drinks.

And Fish Fowler's dad got everyone singing.

Traffic came to a complete stop.

Maggie, who lived near by, came to see what the fuss was about. She couldn't believe her eyes!

We ♥ Maggie

At the same time, the headteacher, Mrs Biggs, came running out to see what was happening.

e Love
aggie

BRING BACK MAGGIE!

Maggie came to her rescue. She picked
up one of the signs and sat Mrs Biggs
(who luckily didn't weigh much)
carefully on top of it. Then she leapt up
behind her. "Hold tight!" she called.

The two of them took off.
They flew over the traffic – over roofs
of cars and bonnets of buses; over vans,
taxis and continental lorries ...

SANDWICH
JUNCTION

... up Myrtle Street, down The Cut and round the bend to Sandwich Junction. There was the ambulance wailing loudly at the end of the long line of traffic.

The ambulance crew whisked
Mrs Biggs off to hospital.

Chapter Five

When she came back to school,
  Mrs Biggs sent for Maggie.
"Maggie," she said, "you saved me
  a great deal of pain and misery.
  What can I do to thank you?"
"Just give me back my crossing,"
  Maggie said.

"I should never have listened to
Mr Watkins," said Mrs Biggs.
"The crossing is yours
for as long as you
want it."

On the day Maggie came back to her crossing, everybody got a lollipop from her back pocket. The children were so happy, they cheered and cheered.

Mr Grudge was sent off to be a Traffic Light Mender. He was happy too because he didn't have to see the children any more.

And Sam Watkins was the happiest of all because everybody wanted to be his friend again.

But Maggie is now very careful
where she turns cartwheels!

Dear Tina,
Sam, Ahmed, Fish,
Mary P. and
everyone else at
Greengage.
    We're having
a great holiday.
The beach is brilliant.
    See you all soon.
    Love
Maggie Magic
    x x   and 🐱   x x

For Alexander, Benedict,
Thomas, Emma
and James

First published 2006 by Walker Books Ltd
87 Vauxhall Walk, London SE11 5HJ

2 4 6 8 10 9 7 5 3 1

Text © 2006 Delia Huddy
Illustrations © 2006 Sue Heap

The right of Delia Huddy and Sue Heap to be identified
as author and illustrator respectively of this work has
been asserted by them in accordance with the
Copyright, Designs and Patents Act 1988

This book has been typeset in Officina Sans

Handlettering by Sue Heap

Printed in China

British Library Cataloguing in Publication Data:
a catalogue record for this book
is available from the British Library

ISBN-13 978-1-84428-929-5
ISBN-10: 1-84428-929-X

www.walkerbooks.co.uk